The

Simple Mechanic

of

Infinite Execution

A Novella

Linda A. Lavid

Full Court Press
Buffalo, New York

Published by Full Court Press
A division of FCPressLLC
Buffalo, NY 14223

ISBN-10: 0-9817070-7-6
ISBN-13: 978-0-9817070-7-5
Library of Congress Control Number: 2013940360

This book is a work of fiction. Incidents, names, characters, and places are products of the author's imagination and used fictitiously. Resemblances to actual locales or events or persons living or dead, is coincidental.

Foreword

This novella is a confluence of impressions I absorbed, deconstructed, and subsequently repurposed from: Calvino's *If on a winter's night a traveler*; telescopic and microscopic renderings of scientific discovery; flotsam of mind-bending definitions such as, but not limited to, consensual rape; neuroscience and pop psychology that, to be honest, I probably misconstrued; the Bible; dreams; meditative sessions; and on the rarest occasion, my actual life. In the beginning, this was a regurgitation on how one develops a sexual identity. In the end, it became about me and my continuing confusion in making sense of this three-dimensional plane. Dear Reader, thanks for joining me. L.

+-o 1 o->

I must cajole you with the word *penis* or the phrase *forcing his lips against hers* so you'll keep reading, so your eyes will sail across the page. It's my job to hold your attention. Trust me, it's not that easy. Distractions abound. You're waiting for the phone to ring. The nurse to call out your name.

It's a game we play, but only if you're willing. I, of course, am always willing. I've been practicing awhile now, lobbing words, sentences, paragraphs. Case in point, I've already written a few sentences and you, vaguely curious, are still reading. Perhaps you'll grace me with another minute of your time and a few more lines of text. That would make me happy. And if you do, I'll give you a story with an ending that will satisfy. Guaranteed.

You smirk. Yeah right. Nevertheless, my hubris entices. Who am I to know what makes you satisfied? We are no relation. But I would disagree. We are very much related, for therein lies the reason why stories are written and read, told and listened to.

Continuing, let me say I'm a naughty girl. Perhaps the word *naughty* tantalizes you with sexual innuendo and playfulness. And a naughty *girl*, takes it one step further to licentiousness. I choose words carefully. I don't want to become boring, predictable. It could be my demise. At any moment you could reach for the remote and flip on the television.

So, I say I'm a naughty girl. And in a split second your mind conjures fleeting images — nakedness and last night or week-end or month when your lover, spouse was on top, panting and slapping against you. I should be embarrassed about such things. I was prudishly raised by church-going parents and a cadre of nuns who covered their bodies in wool and heavily starched cotton. But I am shameless. Holding your attention is everything to me.

However, words are hardly enough. I know my limitations. A shiny hook must be dangled.

This story is about a man and a woman, a boss and a worker bee. They are from different departments, different social strata, different worlds. He drinks top shelf liquor and plays golf at the country club. She line dances to country music between sips of diet Coke and rum. And, as you may suspect, he is ten years older and married.

Like us, their meeting is serendipitous, a matter of being in the same place at the same time. Please note I did not say at the wrong place at the wrong time. I try not to judge or give away too much too soon. Simply we are here while they are there, standing in the company cafeteria ordering sandwiches to go, specifically tuna fish on whole wheat. They are positioned rather close which is surprising since there's no need. It's almost two o'clock in the afternoon and the cafeteria is practically empty.

Imagine stepping back and taking a wide shot of this corporate lunchroom located in the east wing of the seventh floor. One cafeteria worker is on wipe-down duty. She sprays a tabletop, does a quick swipe then moves on. She is the only one making noise as she bumps along rattling tables and chairs. And from this vantage point you are indeed struck by the close proximity of the man and woman who are waiting for sandwiches. In fact, if you didn't know any better, you would assume they were coworkers, friends, or something on that continuum. A sliver of space separates them, but just barely. They are so close, they could whisper. They are so close they could pass state secrets. They are so close, no good is sure to come of it.

And in fact, the first thing he notices is the way she smells, very fresh and clean. Suddenly, he longs to dive into his swimming pool, where the clear water, deceptively blue, washes away the morning's insipid phone calls and asinine questions he had to field with misleading truthfulness. He looks toward the left and tries to get a better sense of her from his peripheral vision. He sees what he seeks—breasts jetting forward, ensconced beneath thin sheaths of cotton and lace; breasts that hang heavy when loosened from their bonds, breasts with dark puckered tits that he can suck and bite. The woman is naked in the pool, attached to him, straddling his waist with her legs. Water swishes between them, making quiet lapping sounds. Her breasts are buoyant, sometimes touching him, sometimes not. And as they rise and fall, the crystalline water glistens....

Dear Reader, to be better oriented please know the woman is sensibly dressed in a white blouse and black straight skirt. Her outfit is cinched at the waist with a wide belt. Her shoes are red with pointed toes and sharp spindly heels. Of this, he is vaguely aware.

From the real world a voice intrudes: Pickle with your sandwich? He nods and reaches for his wallet.

The woman stares at his hands as he fingers the bills inside the fold and without warning a primal feeling, both basic and beyond reason, stirs. Little does she realize how subtle yet unproven confluences affect us all at one time or another.

Consider you and me. On a busy street we walk. I am heading north, while you are going south. We are unknown to each other. Still, my eyes lift from watching the ground and find you, moving quickly with an assured gait. And for whatever reason you turn your head in my direction. Our glances connect in an extraordinary, intimate way until, within the time it takes for light to travel, we blink, disconnect and continue, seemingly untouched.

I believe there are matters not totally understood but insinuated by such events. Perhaps they are caused by gravitational pulls from retrograde planets or auras that bleed then blend becoming colors in the ultraviolet range sensed only by birds. I'm still trying to figure it out. However, what attracts her to him is not his aura. Of that I can assure. His hands are large and tan and muscular; hands reminiscent of others that ran up her leg, traveled along her back, pinned down her wrists.

He pulls out a fifty-dollar bill and calls out to the cashier that he'll pay for everything—his lunch and the woman's too. Oh yes, and keep the change. Money talks, without him having to bother. A lesson learned from his parents and theirs: cash is more than commodity. Always. But that's another story.

Please know, he doesn't buy lunch for women at work. In fact, this is the first time he's ever done so. There are rules talked about in the boardroom, rules between company men that have less to do with propriety than with saving their company's behind from embarrassing lawsuits, rules that, today in this seventh-floor cafeteria, are obviated due to an overriding, growing stiffness between his legs caused by…he can't be sure. The smell of tuna? The deftly handled knife? The thin skin of the tomato that, resistant at first, splits apart oozing juice and seeds? Point is, once the gear shifts, caution blows out the exhaust.

The woman hears his offer. But the overture pales to the sound of his voice, authoritative and assured; so unlike the effusive, fictitious, desperate chatter found in accounts receivable—love the dress, love the shoes, great haircut. A man's voice reverberates. A man's voice buffers and surrounds and draws her under. She'd like to hear it again. Close her eyes and imagine *Take it off* in a deep-throated demand. There's arousal in servitude. In seconds, hormones are released causing a chain of events that leave her mouth dry. And while she tries to focus on his words….

He waits, stock still, vigilant, on the edge. It's all about the hunt and its components: stalk, chase, kill, metaphorically speaking of course. He holds the fifty-dollar bill and waits for some acknowledgment from the woman with breasts. Even the sandwich maker stops and looks up. He's waving money in the air, unsure of his next move. Does he remake the offer, only louder? Does he pretend the words never left his mouth? But salvation arrives. A thank you is heard, he pivots, and for the first time they are face to face.

Dear Reader, think to those daily events when a new person is seen close up. Perhaps you are in a store checkout occupied with a duty to perform—the stacking of cans, boxes, the alignment of bottled, jarred, plastic-wrapped products—until the activity demands discourse. Paper or plastic? Whereupon you look up to find another human being within arm's reach. At first, there's only a simple scan, an impersonal glance, after which your mind may wander. On the other hand, some detail of that person may cause your eyes to linger, to evaluate, to wonder.

She is pretty but plain. No long blond hair to fall over his chest or full red lips to consume his hidden parts. Her hair is of some indiscriminate color he can only guess at—light ash brown? In a style that is wispy, blown about, as if she's just gotten out of bed. Yes, of course. Perhaps that's the attraction, a reminder of how she may look in the privacy of his office, on the leather couch, each pump solid, forceful, with legs wrapped around him and hot breaths against his cheek.

"Sir. Are you listening?"

He snaps back. Two plates with sandwiches, chips and a pickle sit on the counter.

"Your food's ready."

Suddenly, hands, his and hers, reach. And for a moment our couple is in tandem where remarkable, complicated, synaptic messages from hand to spine to brain, and back down again, are repeated in two separate bodies with the same results. They each grab a plate. Without forethought, he says, "Where should we sit?"

The question is a curious one. Certainly polite. But there's an assumption made, a command hidden in the subtext. Still, she could object (How dare you?) or interject (Sorry. Got work.) or scurry off without a response. But truthfully, she likes the panache, the smoothness, the tone of complicity they have yet to share. "Wherever you like," she says.

They weave around the tables and chairs to a distant place where, he hopes, their voices won't carry. Already he's planning a move, not totally formalized. He stops. There's a moment's hesitation, uncertainty. With some parrying, he sits facing the room as she slides in across. Without a word, or a bite, he takes a better look. Sunlight pours over her, exposing fine hair along the side of her face. His gaze then follows a slender neck to where the collar of her blouse fans out. There is no cleavage. Still, her breasts are full and high….

He's framed by glass and the city beyond. But the view pales to his shameless stare. Understanding men, she sits straighter. Yes, they feast with their eyes, take it all in, and frankly, as luck would have it, she likes being appraised, gaped at. Her mind is in two places. In one, she is pleasantly aroused. In another she is removed, thinking how each man has a unique checklist of what he likes, most probably imprinted at an earlier time when his body responded without willfulness to secret events—

looking up a young girl's dress at the playground—and not understanding, but liking, the intrigue it held—the flouncy material giving way to where the legs thickened, the swatch of underpants around the curved backside. Boys react early, that's a fact. First voyeurs, then taunters, then going in for the gusto with dares—I'll show you mine if you show me yours—inching the envelope further each time. Men are like boys, never outgrowing, prescient adolescence with all those hormones either natural or store bought.

His lips move. "Unbutton your blouse," he tells her.

She gives him a wry smile as if to say, yeah right.

He is not amused. "Do it," he says.

He wants something she has. A power play has arisen. Suddenly she feels on the edge of a blade. His eyes are riveted. Slowly, she raises her hand and with deft, playful fingers, toys with the top button of her blouse. He nods. He approves. And with a twist the button loosens.

The top of a white bra is showing with swelling mounds to each side. He likes what he sees, but wants more. "Keep going."

Her head turns slightly.

14

He understands. "Don't look. No one's around."

She focuses back with curious, detached thought—how hard is he? How hard is he willing to get in a seventh-floor lunchroom? She reaches, then lingers at the second button. His breath catches. She then rewards him with yet a third button....

With each inch exposed, his heart revs. Her midriff is flat and tight, making her breasts appear larger than he had expected. He'd like to reach over and rip off what's left. But there's no need. The bra has clasps in the front. He juts out his chin, then whispers, "Show me your tits."

We, you and I, smile at this. He's overplayed his hand, made one too many assumptions, demands. We watch for a sly smile to crease her face or trite words to excuse herself. But she is quiet, solemn. In fact, certain body parts, like his, have swollen to a dull ache. Perhaps it shouldn't be a surprise. They are breathing the same air.

She's almost, but not quite, beyond consequences. She's almost, but not quite, ready to leave. How far will the next move take her? She dives in quickly and unhooks the bra. Spontaneously, cloth splits apart, freeing constricted flesh to cool air. Once exposed, her tits tighten, sending an electrical charge throughout her body. A charge that transfers across the table.

His response is no surprise. He tells her to button up and go with him. She nods. They then stand, and barely able to walk, toss their uneaten lunches into the flap of the trash can. Once out of the cafeteria, the two fall into a rabbit's hole of unchartered land.

Pulling away for moment I'd like to make an argument that neither you nor I are very different from this man or woman. There's a familiar story here. Yes. I know for a fact there have been irrational moments in our lives. Spontaneous events driven by emotion, poor judgment—a slapped, crying child perhaps, or a reckless drive after one too many drinks. Point is what separates us is a gossamer wing, transparent, permeable. We're all human. Anyway, your interest is piqued, as is mine. We are voyeurs in this underground place.

With furtive eyes we search for our couple. Imagine. Zoom to spots where they may be.

The elevator shows no sign of them, not his office or hers. They are not in a restroom. And you are blaming me for leading you down this unnerving path.

But wait.

Beyond the cafeteria, beyond the windows, even beyond the building. Outside to where a panoramic view of the high rise is seen. Imagine with X-ray vision, the stairwell that zigzags from the bottom floor to the top. Close your eyes for a moment and listen. What do you hear? Echoing moans? Gasps for air? Undoubtedly. Now look. Let your eyes follow the stairs as they rise higher to where the noise gets louder. Suddenly...payoff.

She's pinned against the wall, skirt hiked up, straddling. He's deep inside her, pumping quick, short thrusts. They're panting, moaning and well beyond any measure of control. Though close physically, they are deep within their own bodies, where each reptilian brain's insatiable hunger for pleasure and pain must be fed. We watch their contorted faces and understand how wracked their bodies are with exploding hormones, muscles, nerves. The privacy of the matter should be honored, but we do not. We want to experience more, zoom in so close that we can step inside the gyrating unit they share. But just as we make the move, their bodies release deep shivering throbs. And we are left gawking, neither in nor out of the rabbit's hole where the balloon's popped and the movie's over.

But there's more.

Denouement comes quickly for the man and woman. In a heap their bodies loosen. He slides out. She stands. Buttons are fastened, hair is rearranged. Then one heads up the stairs, the other down.

However, matters are quite different for you and me. What we've read has affected us, drawn us inward to a time of similar circumstance. Tell me, what was it like? Loving or rough? Kind or cruel? Generous or scant? Did you strip, suck, slap, bite? Was the rising excitement fed then taken away, over and over again? Or would you like to share an anecdote that's unusually singular—odd, dreamlike, tentative? Interesting how sex is a simple mechanic of infinite execution. Interesting how sex—the thought, picture, sound of it—never gets tired. In any event, before we share stories, let me light two cigarettes and pass one over.

Under normal circumstances the story of the man and the woman would have finished on the previous page. I tend toward the abrupt ending. But I've committed to take the journey further. Not for your sake but for mine. Yes, I do have a horse in the race. Namely me, and a trait I have to experiment, figure things out, tip a coffee cup and watch what happens when drips fall, land, and stream across unlevel surfaces. This is who you're dealing with, an unlikely colleague in a faraway room who becomes enchanted by certain things, specifically, as I have mentioned, you, Dear Reader, and the fine thread of silk that ties our little fingers together. Understand every time I write and tell a story, I also attempt to engage, amuse and generally ingratiate myself to whoever's been kind enough, curious enough, bored enough to read what I've written. Allow me to say entertainment is always a juggling act, not unlike the plate-spinning Ed-Sullivanian bits seen on black and white screens. You see, the guy wasn't just spinning plates, he had a shtick as well, that part where he almost tripped, almost slipped, almost overlooked the fourth plate that wobbled. *Almost* I say because he knew full well what he was doing at every moment. Unfortunately, I haven't quite reached his level of skill. Not yet. Anyway, we writers are wearily troublesome to ourselves, always thinking, asking questions, weighing the consequences. E.L. Doctorow is quoted: *Writers are not just people who sit down and write. They hazard themselves. Every time you compose a book your composition of yourself is at stake.* But I digress.

The story of the man and woman bifurcates. Each returns into the respective streams of their lives. Of course each stream is not the same current they briefly stepped out of ten minutes ago. When events occur, trajectories are affected. It's the law of the universe. Change is ubiquitous, constant and, paradoxically, unchangeable. And amid such endless flux, story evolves.

The man returns to his office by taking the stairs up three flights. At the landing, and before he opens the door into the reception area, he pats his chest pockets. Normally he does this to make sure he has his glasses and phone, neither of which is consequential at this time. What is important, however, is getting from point A to point B, out from this tenth-floor landing and into the confines of his office where he can take a breath, for he is breathing quite heavily at this moment. He suspects the quick climb the cause.

Understand he's a logical man prone to uncomplicated conclusions; a man who sees cause and effect with unfettered vision. Still, allow me to suggest a sweating body can be caused by other conditions, emotional, psychological conditions. Denial, guilt, falsehoods for instance. Or perhaps the machination of a mind to compartmentalize, minimize. You know, that unique ability to take events and relegate them to dark corners of our psyches: frogs blown up for fun, stones thrown off highway overpasses. Events, so inconsequential, they are barely remembered. But such occurrences are never truly forgotten, only placed in boxes where they may or may not remain, for all memories are not created equal. Barometric pressures exist within, and interlocking flaps have their limitations.

In any event, the man has a greater concern at this moment. There's a gauntlet to consider, presided over by a loquacious secretary.

He leans against the wall to steady his breath.

He must be careful of any telltale signs. There's the possibility of lipstick on his collar and a spot or smudge somewhere on his pants. Then there's the matter of scent.

He raises his fingers to his nose. What lingers is unmistakable—an odor with a heavy, dark undertone, part earth, part spice. He breathes it in again. The rush fills the limbic brain where libido lies. His eyes close to its intoxication. He believes the scent is a simple indulgence of insignificant consequence. Little does he know with each inhale, he's bypassing the cortex where logical thoughts reside. Little does he know, basic smells (as innocent as they seem) feed olfactory nerves that impel direct stimuli to a place where powerful emotions merge with memory. Little does he know, as he breathes in her scent, he's playing with fire. He would laugh at this. He's not an animal whose instincts ride him ragged. And in fact, amid the addictive smell, a logical thought does come to mind. Perhaps he should climb another flight of stairs to a freely accessible restroom located on the eleventh floor. There he could wash his hands, slap some water on his face, and dive back into present time. But the thought is dismissed. What's the hurry? And suddenly we realize, by this simple choice, he's doomed on a subconscious level. He reaches for the door.

Past a bank of elevators, he enters a communal area where a familiar crown of graying hair floats above a high counter. He makes a quick right and heads to his inner sanctum.

"Hey, stranger," she calls out. "Where's the fire?

Sliding his hands into pockets, he turns. "Sorry. Got things on my mind."

"I thought you were at lunch."

"Well yes. I—" He stops aware of a complication. Specifically, a line of questioning followed by a line of lies.

"You OK?" She asks in a matronly way.

"I'm fine."

"So. Did you have lunch?"

"I went to the cafeteria."

"That's nice. What did you order?"

A little voice in his brain says *piece of ass.* "Tuna," he says aloud.

"I love their tuna sandwiches. They're the best. Someone said it's because they put sweet relish in them."

"Yeah, I— "

"But I think it's because they're light on the

mayo." Her face scrunches up. "I hate when tuna is swimming in mayo. Just imagine what happens when it gets in your stomach, let alone your arteries."

"I hear ya. Well, I got to get to work now."

"I made coffee. Decaf. Getting late in the afternoon. Can I bring you a cup?"

"No. I'm fine thanks."

"And there are some doughnuts left in the break room. Help yourself. I don't want to take them home. I could freeze them, but the filling gets all gloppy."

Checking his watch, the man hopes to send a clear message that he has urgent business to attend to. The act goes unnoticed.

"The plain doughnuts seem to freeze OK. Peanut sticks, fried cakes. But I really shouldn't even have—" His secretary stops. "Did you do something to your hair?"

He blinks. "Hmm. No."

She gets a quizzical look. "It seems wet or something."

He shrugs. "I just ran up the stairs."

"And your tie's crooked."

She rises. "Let me fix it for you."

He rears back. "Viv. Relax. I got it."

"Don't be silly. I don't mind."

Seconds later her face is inches away from his. Way too close for comfort, way too close to prevent those invisible puffs of scent-riddled molecules into her personal space. His hands close tight inside his pockets.

After several tugs of the tie, she stands back. "There you go. Perfect."

"Thanks," he says. "Listen I have to finish a report. Can you hold my calls?"

She turns away. "No prob."

And in five short steps, he enters his office, closes the door, and heads to the desk. There he collapses. Finally at rest in a place of comfort, he breathes easily, effortlessly and thinks of the woman in the stairwell. Just for a while, he doesn't want to relinquish the memory, have it corrupted or overwritten by outside intrusion. He'd rather stay in a certain frame of mind for as long as feasibly possible where he can relive the sexual encounter that was amazingly uncluttered by emotions, histrionics, pretense. A fuck like no other, dare he say…the perfect fuck.

We smile at this summary for there is danger in such thoughts. Aggrandizement of certain activities is not always recommended, no matter how private and confidential. After all, scurrilous, remarkable acts between two consenting adults are not so grand when subsequent ramifications in the form of breaking headlines are delivered to the door. Ask any politician.

From the bottom drawer, he pulls out a fifth of vodka and takes a swig, partly in celebration, partly to blur the harsh reality that he remains at work. He then rolls back his chair, reclines, and places his feet on the desk. With closed eyes, he replays the moments of the indiscretion, calling to mind how it felt to be exploring unfamiliar territory. He cups his hand over his clothed penis and watches the internal movie.

From our perspective, we see a man at rest with a hint of a smile on his face. He looks calm and serene, but where he takes himself is anything but.

Dear Reader, at this junction, an introduction is in order. Meet Michael Jones, age forty-five, married for twenty years to Caitlyn, a girl he had met in a Spanish class at college. *Hola Miguel, Hola Catalina*, were the first words spoken between them. He felt stupid, uncomfortable, but she laughed. They went for coffee and the course was set.

He has two teenage girls, both in high school. He often feels an outsider at home and has gained, in his opinion, too much knowledge of things feminine.

On the other hand, being the only alpha male within the confines of a sprawling four-bedroom, three-and-a-half bath Tudor, he enjoys the attention and fuss on his birthday even though he always foots the bill. He would describe himself as happily married.

But these facts are external. There's a unique person in all of us and describing anyone with tiresome details lacks punch. Better to relate a secret he shamefully carries.

His first sexual experience, or better stated, arousal, was at age seven. His parents were getting ready to go out for dinner and he was standing at the door to their bedroom. His father was in the shower and his mother, naked, was walking around. It was the first time he had ever seen her without clothes. She had something missing between her legs but made up for it with her protruding breasts that hung heavily. His response to seeing her naked was surprising and immediate. He turned away from the door and in the darkened hallway pulled down his pants. His penis was sticking straight out. He poked it. It gave a resilient bounce. He then pulled up his pants and looked back into the room.

His mother was then seated at the vanity where a string of lights ran along the sides and top. She and her breasts were illuminated, glowing. She pressed a large white puff along her neck and beneath each arm, then pushed up each breast, and powdered below and between. From where he stood, he smelled the familiar scent when she tucked him in bed.

Once finished, she sat straighter and turned her face from side to side. Then oddly, she placed a finger in her mouth, like a Popsicle stick, and sucked. Seconds later, her wet fingertip circled each tit. The stirring in Michael's pants felt thicker, stronger, better. He thought of rechecking the situation, when a disquieting moment occurred. In the brightly lit, mirrored reflection, his mother's eyes locked with his. He froze under her unblinking stare and waited for a scolding. Nothing came. They only looked at one another until his father's voice called out, "Where's the goddamn razor?" It was then that his mother's attention disengaged. It was then that he stepped into the shadows and ran to his room.

For years he wondered what actually happened that evening. In high school, after learning about the Oedipus complex, he figured Freud may have hit the nail on the head. Later, after having children, he had second thoughts about his mother and suspected some dark motives on her part. It's a mystery and secret (part shame, part complicity) he carries. Join the party.

In any event, this first sexual encounter has haunted him. Amazing for a two-minute span of time that occurred by accident, where there was no premeditation, no exploitation, no subjugation, just a wordless, sanitized episode of watching. Perhaps, such is a testament to the sexual powers of opposite-sex parents. But there's more. The event described created three long-term concrete ramifications. For one, he's a diehard breast man. Secondly, he holds an affinity for baby powder. Thirdly, he doesn't totally trust women.

A knock on the door awakens him. He sits up. His secretary pokes in her head. "Going now. Have a nice evening."

He smiles. "Any calls?"

"Yes. A woman. No name. No message. Said she'd call back."

"When did she phone?"

"Just a minute ago."

Barely perceptible, he feels a tinge in his stomach. "Did she sound familiar?"

"No."

"What did you tell her?"

"Since it was getting late, I told her you had already left for the day. Was that OK?" she asks.

"Sure."

"Okey, dokey then. Have a nice evening. See you tomorrow."

"Yes," he says as his secretary leaves and a surfacing preoccupation comes to the fore.

Michael Jones now admits where there is cause, there is effect; where there is action, there is consequence; and where there are dreams there are nightmares. Yes, sinewy, entangling tentacles that reach up from the ground, grab him by the ankles, and drag him back into this present world where sinister possibilities lie—accusations, blackmail, public hearings, joblessness, divorce, destitution.

But he's not to be played. There's a simple way out. Complete denial. After all, it's his word against hers. Yes. Clearly. And he relaxes back into the chair with only one remnant of concern: a wisp of guilt. Terrain past traveled.

He slumps over the keyboard, goes to Google, searches for florists, and sends a dozen red roses to his home with a message, *Love you a bunch*. Satisfied, he downs a last swig of vodka and heads over to the lavatory. Five minutes later, he's exiting the elevator on the third floor where he trots over the above-ground walkway that leads to the parking ramp.

Amid the exiting stream of people, his pace is

brisk and furtive. And suddenly, we are reminded of another scenario, a man who, having tasted the forbidden fruit, was cast into darkness and where life, as he had known it, changed. Of course such a man did not travel alone. He had an accomplice.

+-o 3 o->

Her name is Kristin.

After the event, she descends three flights of stairs, enters a Ladies Room, soaps ups several paper towels, and enters a far stall. There she hikes up her skirt, pulls down her panties, and wipes away the remnants of bodily fluids, still viscous, warm, and running down her leg. She then sits on the toilet and pees.

Mingled in the hot stream, she senses vapor perhaps the respondent gas formed by the forging of two elements stirred by heat and friction, seeping from her body into the cool atmosphere, where, she suspects, constricted molecules, part ways and separate into their original state of plumpness and singular identity. The nature of such elements, she imagines, are opposite and opposing. They are of maleness, femaleness, microscopic arrows and circles that repel and attract in endless maneuverings, replaying over millennia, throughout cultures, when boy meets girl and crazy things happen.

But such are her momentary thoughts, fleeting, barely above consciousness. There are more pressing matters to consider. Matters having to do with homeostasis, that nature to have stability return after peaks of disquieting activity.

Already her body is wilting, played out, depleted. And with bravado, she is tempted to assume the event is without consequence, a dalliance to recall when she's old and in some derelict state of cognition where one's experience of past and present events is a jumbled affair. Tempted, I reiterate, for certain acts of recklessness have magnetic properties that seduce. Case in point, addictive joyrides where anticipation, fear, excitement merge with rocking, jolting velocity, pounding beats, visual spin, and where loaded sensory explosions brand themselves into the brain, across hemispheres and through levels of jellied cortices and lobes, never to be forgotten. Poor girl may be doomed.

In any event, Kristin stands, crumples up a wad of toilet paper, and places it into the crotch of her panties. Just in case. She then lowers her skirt and lifts the small metal latch.

At the full-length mirror, she takes a good look at herself, half expecting some change, some telltale sign of the indiscretion. But all she sees, remarkably, is a clear-eyed woman. I say *remarkably* because she is judge and jury when it comes to her appearance and rarely is the muster passed.

She moves closer to the reflection. There is no negative chatter in her head, just a curious look into her own eyes with their gray specks. How quickly she's stepped out from the current and onto solid ground. She checks her watch. Barely a half hour has passed since she had left to go to lunch.

Then it happens, a slight bubble to the surface—slut. A familiar word that has transmigrated throughout her life, a word that, over the years, mutated into various meanings, at times nuanced with amusement, at other times much less so. Her smile is wry, Mona Lisa-ic. She challenges her own gaze. *Whatever.* And thinks about her lips. Should she go for cherry red or shimmery bronze?

As Kristin regains position in the current of her workday, we may, having been privy to her behavior, come to some conclusions, perhaps not terribly favorable, of who she is. We may even point accusing fingers in the ascending order of vamp, bitch, whore, cunt. But I would suggest, we (yes, even myself for I am experiencing Kristin as a ghost-like figure with feathery edges who rises from the vast netherworld of my subconscious) keep our minds open. People are rarely what we assume despite our insistent and inept perceptions, interpretations, prejudices. Case in point and juxtaposition: Theodore Robert Cowell, aka Ted Bundy, the boyishly grinning lawyer, a Burberry kind of guy who parents, police, even women considered pedigreed. Until the bludgeoning. Way to go Teddy.

So we consider Kristin with an open mind. We even step into her brain for a glimpse.

Again *slut* is heard inside her head. But this time the voice isn't hers. It belongs to Jimmie, her mother's old boyfriend who, when Kristin was eleven, began referring to her with endearments previously only reserved for her mother. "Slut," he'd told Kristin when she walked into the kitchen wearing a new pair of jeans and cowboy boots. "You look like a slut. Just like your mother." In reaction, she ran blindly out the door, then deep into the yard behind the garage. Tears of shame, of guilt, of having a body, of wanting to take a knife and drive it into his sorry soul, flooded her vision.

Now, in recollection, a subtle change takes place. If you look closely, you'll see the trembling of her lower lip. *Slut*

And we are reminded how our lives are not linear paths from birth to death, but composed of experiential hodgepodge, imprints that push, yank, trail and taunt us. Past moments to be lived over and over by wild subterranean connectives that surface and bleep into our consciousness, serving as a reminder that while one can run, one can not hide. But such is the human condition. Oh Happy Days. Still, with practice such toxic sludge can be re-boxed, reframed, or temporarily unremembered by pharmaceuticals, alcohol, or a real crazy bitchin' rant.

Kristin shakes her head, resets and rallies (she survives as we all do) and moves closer to the mirror. Yes, some refresh of mascara would be nice. And she burrows through her purse.

By age fourteen, dear Jimmie had upped the raunchiness. In drunken stupors, and when Kristin's mother was out of the room, he'd approach her from behind, breath on her neck and say, "You need to be tied up." And part of her believed she did.

The intervening years had transformed Kristin. Childhood innocence eroded into a curious blend of vanity and insecurity. While the stage was set with Jimmie, it took on steam with boys at school, "You need to be fucked" and men in cars with their pants unzipped, "Hey you. Come over here." Embracing the mantle of slut, she then colored her hair blonder and filled drawers with push-up bras and scant lace undies. Attention, no matter the kind, took precedence as she free-fell into slut-dom and puberty. Sound familiar?

In any event, knowing Kristin's history, you might assume a rap sheet of peccadilloes similar to her recent indiscretion. But in fact, she has never done this before. At least not in this particular way, place, time. Yes. There were some occasions of poor judgment late at night after shots, chasers and a slow dance. (Let's face it, who among us can cast the first stone as far as that goes?) But in daylight? Of sound mind? At work? No. This was a first, and first times always pack a punch especially when orgasms are involved.

So what led her to do it? Allow me to fill in some blanks.

Directly after leaving the cafeteria, once they cleared the doorway, he cradled her elbow into the crook of his arm. It was a simple act, reminiscent of a gentleman helping a gentlewoman across a slick cobblestone street. The grasp was light, barely perceptible. There was the thought to pull away, but to be frank, she felt weak, untethered, possibly from some blood pressure anomaly, possibly from the stark fluorescent lighting that rasped against her internal state of arousal. It was as if she'd just come out of a movie theater or a dream, somewhat disoriented by the lights and goings on. But then again, not much was going on. The hall was empty, noiseless, except for their shoes on the linoleum, her clippity-clack, his shuffling step. At least that was her recollection. Anyway, it only seemed natural, given the circumstances, to lean into his solid, moving musculature, when, in response, he held tighter.

And so began their *pas de deux* where segments of personal space were no longer and specific points of contact intensified.

Through layers of material—her bloused arm, his suited jacket—she felt undulating movement and heat. Hers? His? The combination of both? She wasn't sure. She could have walked for hours that way, unaware that leaning into a stranger is a seduction, a gesture that falsely implies: if you fall, I'll catch you; if you need me, I'll be there. Yes. See the problem? An unspoken covenant between strangers is dangerous territory should assumptions be made. A supportive arm is a supportive arm. Nothing more. Still who can blame her for the momentary slip into a comforting fantasy? It's how we all get through the day.

Her usual trip to the lunchroom was a quick right from the elevator, down a short hall where the familiar steamy smell of soup (tomato? chicken noodle?) often hung in the air. But that area was well behind. They had already traveled one corridor, turned, and continued on.

If she had chosen to pay attention, she would have noticed a line of open doors to the left and right. If she had chosen, she could have stopped and looked into the offices and seen how the strip of overheads cast a bluish light onto half-walled, wired-up cubicles, configured in a maze where workers punched on keyboards, watched the clock, and played discreet games of Solitaire, Hearts, Free Cell. If she had chosen....

But her interest was consumed by the hallway itself, how it led in one direction—forward—and how she was willing to step, one foot after another, with a strange man. She could have pulled away, reared back, but for what godforsaken reason? To return to work and the cloying atmosphere of chugging copiers, ringing phones, useless chatter? No. She felt on a blade of an intriguing curve, a five-degree turn that seduced her gently to the side, where the gravitational pull lessened and time warped back into itself. No past, no future, only the moment.

They approached a heavy metal exit door. He stepped ahead and pushed down hard on the metal bar. The noise was loud, echoing, jarring. As if a schoolboy about to be caught for some mischievous act, he glanced behind her. Whatever his eyes searched for didn't stop him from grabbing her arm tighter and moving her forward. But at the portal, she stopped.

Dear Reader, there always comes a time in couplings where maneuverings become tentative. Fact is, no two bodies can remain aligned for very long. At every level of existence from minuscule quarks to expanding universes, there is one truth— endless movement—caused by forces of many kinds and measures. In the human realm such movement is further complicated by intrusive thoughts and feelings. Let's face it, how anyone gets together is miraculous. So what exactly made her stop?

It was atmospheric. When the door to the stairwell opened, a rush of hot, gummy air pressed against her. Trapped in dense, smothering, unbreathable space, a primordial response took over. Frozen to the spot, like a female in the wild, driven by instinct and an overload of adrenaline, she became alerted to the options. Fight or flight? And a quick subliminal realization surfaced—if she wanted to get away, how fast and far could she run? Or worse, would anyone hear her screams?

Yes. Crazy thoughts abound when violent images are fed to greedy, fearful eyes nightly. But then again, bad things do happen. Victims are not always actors. Often enough they are real, some in the wrong place, others with the wrong people, and more still who are just asking for it. A brutal rape in an office stairwell would raise questions. Had he dragged her in? No. Pointed a gun at her head? No. Pulled a knife and snipped off each button one by one? No. But violence comes in many ways. As does injury. He could force her on her knees and rip out her tonsils. Fat chance for any sympathy there. And we are reminded how victims are accused harbingers of their own fate.

In any event, at the portal into the stairwell, whatever charms he had no longer took precedence. Even her arousal seemed secondary. It was then that she needed a reason, a rationalization to continue. "Why should I go with you?"

He smiled. "Because you're beautiful."

And while we are won over by pretty words, Kristin is not. Compliments are fluff, short cuts, skeleton keys in pockets that open doors, spread legs.

She is not so inexperienced, so gullible, so desperate for a gnawed, tired bone. And for the first time, with complicity stalled, she challenged him. "You'll have to do better than that."

His eyes turned downward, skittering back and forth. She, sufficiently cooled, detached, became amused. What rummaged words, expressions will work their magic? His glance jerked back up. He had an idea. "I want to fuck you".

Not bad, she considered. After all being desired trumps pretty words. Still, she held her ground. For an eternity they looked into each others eyes. Then closing into her ear, he whispered, "Let's fly." And on her tongue, dark chocolate melted. She then stepped across the threshold and into the heat.

The door to the bathroom opens.

"Hey, Kristin."

It's her coworker D'arcy. "Hey."

"You missed the excitement. Julia had a fight with Justin."

"D'arcy. They're always arguing."

"No. This is different. The wedding's canceled. Julia was off the hook. He came down to talk to her. She called him a dog. He must have cheated on her. She walked out. Didn't even ask for permission. Mr. Bowles is trying her cell."

"Just more drama."

"How can you say that! I thought she was your friend."

Kristin dries her hands. "They shouldn't get married if they can't stop fighting."

D'arcy shrugs. "I suppose. Just back from lunch?"

"Sort of."

"Did you go shopping?"

"No.

"So you went for a walk?"

Kristin's eyes settle on the office gossip girl. Suddenly Kristin has a secret, a private golden nugget for her to hide, call her own, fall under its spell.

In the lapse of silence, D'arcy turns to the mirror. "I wonder if she'll get fired? You just can't walk out on a job."

Kristin pumps another round of soap onto her hands and froths them up. Five minutes later, she's back at her desk answering a call from Chicago. There's an overcharge in the account. Her fingers fly over the keyboard. Columns flash across the screen. Her glance rolls down. Yes. An extra zero has been added. Once corrected, a deep voice, no longer irritated, says "Thanks."

After hanging up, she reaches for a tin of Altoids and cracks open the metal lip. While unfolding the papery pocket, her glance cuts to the clock. In a matter of forty minutes she has accommodated two men. Yep, she smiles to herself, always giving, never taking.

Michael Jones's life is clean and orderly as noted by his car, a leased upgraded Prius, that is weekly washed on the outside, monthly vacuumed, spritzed, sanitized on the inside, just like his house and body and mouth, although time frames differ.

May I suggest the routines of our lives are telling. No need to see a psychoanalyst or psychic to understand the truths of any one of us. Take any behavioral trait and get a glimpse into the whole. However, what's even more interesting, curious, and worthy of note, are the divergences. In fact, just yesterday, Michael tossed a gum wrapper onto the passenger seat where it remains at this moment, an odd little crumpled ball of paper sitting all lonesome in an otherwise showroom interior. He may have been distracted. On the other hand....

Where there is order, there is chaos. Where

there is control, there is powerlessness. And in between there are mechanics that oscillate, hover, cross axes, never to rest. It's a delicate balance better accepted than manipulated. Control and order can not be maintained since chaos and powerlessness are parts of the equation, opposite sides of the same coin. Perhaps Michael has accepted this theory. Perhaps Michael felt the tug of chaos and allowed it to let off steam by allowing a crumpled piece of paper to fall onto the leather seat beside him. On the other hand, it could have been a simple oversight.

Michael's car is traveling north on the 190, with the river to the left and city on the right. He doesn't notice the diamond-like sparkles glistening off the water or the plump curlicue graffiti that interrupts the spanning concrete embankments. He remains in the dream, complimented by being slightly inebriated and pleasantly drowsy. The movement of the car is cradling, the leather seats cushy and soft. He steps on the accelerator every few minutes to feel some velocity, some pull reminiscent of a swelling penis. Well, not just any swelling penis but his. And he marvels how it has rarely let him down, a miracle of nature, a blessing. He smiles, swerves behind a slow moving Camry, and gets back in line. He, now, after a few hours of distraction, is ready to enter the normal parameters of his life and head home.

Heading home. A daily event. Home, like a mantra, a hum that soothes all that ails. Of course *home* is many things to many people. For some, it is a place of light, of comfort, of conversation. For others, it's a place of silence, of slamming doors, of bottles, pills, of irregular hours. Michael Jones is one of the lucky ones though. Home for him is smooth sailing, mostly. While hormonal swings of his wife and two daughters cause the occasional dramatic incident, he has a den with a 48" flat screen, surround sound, and bottles of bonded liquor to weather storms.

Ready to jump into home, he now thinks of the day of the week and considers what he'd like to watch on TV. He likes sports and hot movies. Particularly basketball and soft porn with sex-starved women willing to please. He smiles, distracted by a remembered visual of a hungry mouth.

Alas, the pornography story. It's in us all. Perhaps, Dear Reader, you bristle. Me? No way. But let's be frank. Never ever have stirrings occurred by a picture, a video? Hmm.

Getting back to Michael, his initiation into pornography was singular to those of his peers. It happened in the least expected way on a rainy summer afternoon in his grandfather's country home, a gentleman's farm, where the help was baking black raspberry pies.

His father's father was on the porch smoking. Tall, lean, and mostly laconic, he still showed interest in Michael, always asking the perfunctory, "How's school going?" He himself was an educated man, a doctor, who also invested. A man of many interests with a library to prove it.

On this particular day, with a summer rain slapping on the porch roof and falling in sheets along the railings, he had asked Michael about girls and what he'd thought of them. Michael was ten. He shrugged. His grandfather then asked him to go into the library and get more pipe tobacco. It was located on the desk, near the telephone. No hurry.

What Michael found on the desk was an opened book held in position by the heavy, sheathed Samurai sword purchased on one of his grandfather's trips to Japan. A sword he had often played with. But on this day, his attention was drawn to the opened book where there was a picture, a drawing, with captions not in any language he could read. Not that the picture needed translation. A naked woman lay on a bed. Her legs were splayed, with feet and legs high in the air. A standing man, with his pants down, had an erect penis pointing toward the woman's wide-apart legs. To the side a monk stood. His robes were raised, his large fist grasping an even larger penis. And toward the back, another man watched.

Michael's reaction was first of curiosity. What's going on here? But as he looked more closely his fleeting eyes turned greedy.

When someone sees something for the very first time, when there are no known reference points in memory, the full impact of that visual event is not experienced immediately. Parts are first considered, made sense of, then the connecting begins.

In this case, Michael first recognized the familiar—the man's round bare cheeks and large penis, a penis that resembled his, protruding when he rubbed it. His eyes then went to the woman and how she was lying so openly. What if, he thought, what if that man put his penis inside her? He pulled his face closer to the drawing. Yes, there was a spot, a hole, between her legs. And that thought was instantaneously felt below, inside his shorts.

Suddenly, he grasped the meaning of the picture. This was sex he was seeing. His mouth became dry. His heart raced. He looked at the monk and understood even more. Rubbing his penis wasn't enough, he needed to grab it tight.

And so inside his grandfather's den on a rainy summer afternoon, Michael reached for his penis, surrounded it with curled fingers, looked between the woman's legs and, entering virgin territory, jerked-off for the first time.

The experience was a curious blend of pleasure and fear, like being on a roller coaster only it happened down below. Each squeeze, each yank, stiffened him harder, bigger, and felt better. What was happening here? Was he hurting himself? There was the burning, the pressure, the numbness in his legs. There was also the thought to stop, but no possible way to stop. He was doomed, rising on a ninety-degree track, pushing higher, driving harder. When suddenly, without warning, the apex was reached and a quick, dry, but throbbing release sent shivers throughout his body.

Five minutes later, back on the porch, he had forgotten the tobacco. His grandfather smiled. "Have any questions?" Michael shook his head. His grandfather peered into the sky, "Rain's lightening up. Good for fishing."

During subsequent trips to his grandfather's home, Michael often visited the library. The book had been re-shelved among others. And so began his voyeuristic forays into humping, spanking, sucking bodies complemented with jerk-offs and unusual props that luckily didn't damage his penis. Years later when they cleared out the house, the original book was nowhere to be found. He didn't bother saving any of the others. A first car can never be replaced.

Pulling into the driveway, Michael checks himself in the mirror. There are no surprises. Hair's combed, a stubble's brewing, and his tie remains straight. He nods to himself. For any lingering remnants, he'll dive into the pool where the chlorine will cleanse him squeaky clean. And no one will be the wiser.

With expectations met and a plan in place, he empties out of the car, thereby exiting his work life and entering his family life—a life of swims, cook-outs, and Cohiba Robustos, loving hand-wrapped in Cuba, ordered on-line from Switzerland, and shipped sans their identifying bands.

We follow Michael, a suited, tall, confident man with an easy gait, as he collects the nightly newspaper from the manicured lawn, waves to a neighbor two doors down, and slips inside his home.

In the living room, his younger daughter is practicing the piano. "Hello, Daddy," she says.

Michael grins. "Hey pumpkin."

And instantaneously, without awareness, his blood pressure drops. He is home, safe, secure and ready to savor the evening routine.

To digress for a moment, routines in our lives serve purpose. They are anchoring events that sooth and buffer us from those unsettling moments that tend to throw us into uncertainty, disorder, and, for some, heart attacks. The lowly routine is rarely given its due. Simple repetitive acts go unnoticed, but they are the rhythms of our lives. Needless to say, it's helpful to have routines that are healthy—sleeping regular hours, eating six servings of vegetables daily. Conversely, it's detrimental to have routines that are sabotaging—smoking cigars, having sex with strangers.

I suspect Michael would chide me for this observation. His journeys into unfamiliar territories are hardly routine. But I would argue. Routines are not necessarily daily events. They could happen twice a year, like a routine dentist appointment.

At this, he would smile, perhaps nod. "Yes. You may be right. But it serves a purpose."

"A purpose?" I say.

"A manly purpose," he responds. "Call of nature. There is woman. There is man. And there's really no harm."

It's my turn to nod. "Tell that to your doctor when certain viruses burrow under your skin or bacteria travels up your urethra or tainted bodily fluids do a shock-and-awe number on your T-cells."

Again he thinks about taking that short swim.

Caitlyn, his wife, is in the kitchen. She's petite, blond, and a grand cook who loves spices and wine. "Hi, Honey."

Michael smiles. "What's up Babe?" Normally, he gives her a peck. But today he stands back and explains, "I'm all sweaty. Gonna take a quick dive."

"No prob. Dinner won't be ready for another twenty minutes. Doing that Thai dish you love."

Michael sniffs the air. "Mmm. Can't wait."

She turns back to the stove. His eyes run the length of her, a body of perfect symmetry even in a crisp white shirt, belted jeans, and flats. He particularly loves her ass, the roundest and softest part of her body. (Her breasts are fine. Just a wee bit small.) Anyway, his friends are envious. She's got a great bod *and* she's a great cook. Almost a trifecta. *Almost*, I say, because she is prone to headaches, migraines. He's been told—via her, via her doctor—it's hormonal and there's nothing to be done except manage. Poor thing.

As he watches her, a visual flash sparks inside

his brain and he is back to earlier in the day when he watched his penis pump in and out of the woman, when he felt her tight wetness grip, when he heard her moan, when he smelled their sex. Thoughts, who can stop them? Of course these aren't thoughts, but memories. Memories that have sprouted roots, entangling and engaging different parts of his brain. He pulls his eyes off his wife's ass, shrugs, and heads up the stairs.

In the en-suite bath, he strips down and looks at his reflection. He is happy with what he sees. Nothing has changed much over the years. Sure there are a few extra pounds around his waist, but his shoulders remain broad, and he still has the stamina to swim, shoot hoops, and perform.

Flaccid, amid a patch of hair, his penis is napping. The personified penis—Big Guy, Little Soldier, Captain Winkie—and friend. A friend for not just him but for women to cradle, crave and treat with wanton desire. Well, some women anyway. Like those in videos, sucking cocks. Man. Nothing's hotter. His wife's accommodating on occasions but there's a limit. Besides he doesn't really want to kiss a woman with his cum in her mouth. Does he?

Interrupting his reverie, a car door slams. He walks to the window and looks down. A floristry van is in the driveway. The flowers have arrived—his ticket to assuage any remnants of guilt, his statement to his babe that she's the best. He slips into trunks, grabs a towel, and heads to the pool. He wants his wife to be surprised when she opens the door.

For Michael Jones, swimming is a meditation, a repose from the incessant demands of his job where, at times, he is wrongfully maligned, disregarded, misunderstood, or taken for granted. But such is the way of middle management, a precarious position centered between forces, above and below, where one must maintain the chain of command with the occasional lie or subterfuge to keep everyone happy, albeit in the dark. Suffice it to say, Michael is good at keeping secrets.

At the pool's edge with curled toes hugging the rim, he bends over, raises his arms, sucks in air, and dives in. The shock of the cold water is barely felt as he, like a knife through butter, cuts into the surface tension with barely a splash. When his hands hit bottom, he levels out and strokes parallel to the pool's floor where, in the middle, he stops, becoming a dark shadow, a large bottom feeder, hovering in deep water with only the occasional kick and flailing arm to keep steady and immersed.

We can't see that his eyes are open and he's

mesmerized by silent wavering water, a saturated turquoise blue. We can't understand how submersion into buoyant weightlessness, Michael's second skin, has far more to do with freedom than fear. But most surprisingly, as he hangs airless, we can't imagine that Michael feels like a bird high in the sky where the world's a blue marble and he's traveling at warp speed to a distant nebula of exploding gases and dust.

Seconds wear on and we wonder if emergency action will be needed. But when the last bit of breath is expelled, he turns upward and, with a powerful stroke and kick, surges through the water's surface. Back on planet Earth, he begins his swim, a slow rhythmic crawl from end to end, resetting his biorhythms into their proper sine waves of activity and rest.

After twenty laps, he emerges into the warm evening with beads of water on his skin. He towels off the glistening drops and any lingering molecules left by another person. The past has officially receded to its rightful position—done and over.

Entering the kitchen, the delivered flowers, in a voluminous papered bundle, remain wrapped. They are sitting moored on the kitchen counter. His wife is nowhere in sight. He listens. Her voice is coming from the den. He pads along the hall and stops when he overhears.

"He's done it again," she says.

Who's done what? he wonders.

"How stupid does he think I am?"

Michael smiles. She must be talking to her sister about their father.

"I don't know." Her voice wavers. "It may be time for that convertible."

Convertible? That Mini Cooper she's been talking about? The chords on the piano are loud and annoying. His leans forward and turns his head to hear more clearly. He doesn't realize he's stopped breathing.

"Flowers. My ass.

His mind is moving quickly, tallying up previous indiscretions. Flowers? Yes.

She continues to speak but it's gibberish, streams of words without spaces, vowels. Air pressure, too thick to breathe, presses against his chest. Michael reaches for the door jamb to stay upright, to suck in air, to tell himself it's all right. What he's realizing we already know—when the trickster is tricked, the joke fails to be funny.

Suddenly, Michael's a foreigner in his own home. Nothing is familiar. Welcome to the Land of

Oz.

+-o 5 o->

At 6 PM, we find Kristin in sweats at home sitting on the sofa. She's pressing the TV remote for something amusing. The screen flashes by with annoying thumps of monosyllabic utterings that could be words, animal grunts or extrapolated bites of God- or man-made disasters. (Howling winds? Semi-automatic fire?) Who can tell as images scud by with just enough time for her to evaluate, tap her finger, and move on. If she doesn't find something soon, there are two hundred channels to go, meaning the microwaved fettuccine in a light Alfredo sauce with roasted red pepper and pine nuts is certain to cool to room temperature.

Passing on a *Friends* rerun, Kristin pauses at the local evening news. "Coming up," the anchor says, "Five ways to use less gas." She puts down the remote, grabs the fork, and takes a bite. After a few methodical chews and a swallow, she sighs, acquiescing to another humdrum evening.

Yes. A single woman's life tends to be habitual. I suspect it's a matter of having fewer variables, that is to say interruptions, caused by demanding children, husbands, and the losing battle of staying one step ahead of nature's incessant *désordre*—dirt, dust, hairiness; and two steps ahead of household management duties where the clock is always ticking and, Kristin's counterpart, the married woman, is always running.

However, having taken a hairpin turn by fucking a stranger at work, Kristin's day is not habitual.

Every so often, she puts down the fork and stares into space, like a zombie. Poor girl. Has she been traumatized after the fact? Does she feel used, minimized, objectified? Is she taking the rap for being a wanton slut? I want to tell her it takes two to tango. She glances in my direction and smiles sweetly, vacuously, like a bridesmaid. The woman is hard to read.

"No harm, no foul," I say. After all, there's no real damage, just a brief collision of slapping flesh that will either remain her secret or be unremembered after a Saturday of shoe shopping. I expect a smile but she shrugs me off and looks down. Her eyes skitter back and forth. Hmm.

Theories abound about eye movements and how they indicate if a person is recalling, abstracting, imagining, lying, or, well, having a seizure. It's a matter of an observer being observant, watching carefully, checking for telltale, subtle signs. Of course, Kristin can't forever be an enigma. In the final analysis, she is me and I am her in this land of character creation and dreams. Similar, Dear Reader, to your own nightly meanderings in the subconscious land of slumber and REMs, where odd scenarios and people jumble about helter skelter without rhyme or reason. And where such mysteries are made infinitely clearer when we realize those nightly impressions are simply subconscious parts of ourselves demanding expression. Yes, we are always both the tormentor and tormentee. A troubling truth of sobering proportions.

But back to Kristin. Her eyes are darting side to side as if watching a movie. Now I understand. Instead of moving forward, looking ahead, she's backpedaling into her past as women tend to do. Damn. She's succumbing to that feminine nature where the difference between the sexes goes beyond hormones, body parts, muscle/fat ratios but how each gender perceives the flow of life in the stream of time, that is to say forward or backward, living in the future or living in the past, where events once experienced are conveniently forgotten (male trait) or tiresomely remembered (female trait).

To illustrate, though not necessarily prove my theory, consider the MacBeths, the reckless impulsive husband conjoined to a wife lost in a maze of repetitive hand-washing. Or George and Martha, where one drinks to unremember, and the other drinks to not forget. And we think about the uncanny similarities in our own narratives. Dear Reader, how do we ever survive this maze of earthly existence? Anyway...

Kristin is in a remembering state—a bike trip to the creek with Rob, her first boyfriend. Lying deep inside the crinoline curtain of willow branches, they are kissing, grappling, laughing, whispering. And where for the first time, she sees a stiff penis. "Want to touch it?" he says. It feels like smooth hard rubber.

And I am left wondering what any of this has to do with her day. Perhaps she doesn't have a clue. Memories are not just of events. They are of feelings. Feelings that go beyond remembering where they are instead locked inside body parts—racing hearts, air too thick to breathe, swollen, glutted organs—which could explain a fair amount. On the other hand maybe it's a subconscious connection of similar first times—a tryst in the woods jumbled with a wham-bam in the stairwell at work. Another conclusion could be that her mind is simply wandering.

Before long the news is over and Kristin becomes aware that the how-to-use-less-gas segment has gotten away from her. The sports roundup is now in full swing and instead of watching a remarkable arcing three-point shot taken from center court, her eyes follow the billowing shorts of a player running across court. And she recalls another memory, an affair, eight months earlier, with Jason, her running neighbor, whose girlfriend left.

They, she and Jason, had become acquainted after several incidents of opening and holding the front door as bags, furniture were heaved up the steps and juggled into the vestibule. At the time, and unknown to Kristin, the affair had a two-week shelf life. The girlfriend hadn't really left but had gone to visit her family. It was the other woman who, upon her return, came bouncing down from the third floor. "Hello there. Great to be home." Kristin was confused but still managed "Home?" "Yes, I went to visit my family for our annual trip to Maine." Again, Kristin's response was echolalic, "Maine?" "Hey, thanks for keeping Jay company." Company? And the woman barreled out the front door.

In response, Kristin wobbled into her apartment and headed for the ice cream. By the time the carton was pounded down, she swore off runners and concentrated on Jason's shortcomings: a lying snake who was overly fond of being naked which translated, ninety percent of the time, to seeing his penis flop about like a little-boy-lost. It didn't end there. For several months, Kristin received drunk calls in the early morning hours suggesting he stop by her apartment before heading up the stairs. She had tried to be tactful, but the last attempt was at 5 AM. "Jason," she told him. "Please, stop calling. You come too quick. Sorry." Her words were met with silence. At last, one lie canceled out the other, and there was mutual closure. Byeee.

And so goes the life of a bachelorette—hours of mundane activity sandwiched between ships passing, anchors dropped, and the interminable return to sea where other waters, shores, and moorings are anticipated, sampled and subsequently cut loose. Good news though. Kristin is getting the hang of it.

In the intervening years between Rob and Jason, there was an unemployed poet, misunderstood and uncompensated for his brilliance; a vegan Deadhead with an uninspired vocabulary (dude, like, sweet, man); a born and raised New York State cowboy-boot guy who, she suspected, may have been leaning toward the other team; a girlfriend's ex who felt swapping was as good as the real thing only to pine away and recall endless anecdotal events from the previous relationship; a stalwart, angry, and often drunk uniform wearer (cop by day, security guard by night) who, while her best lover, was one mean motherfucker.

Add this to all that preceded (Jimmie, her mother's boyfriend) through today (whoever he is), she's survived without too much trauma. Granted while there has been a fair amount of confusion, doubt, anger, other- and self-loathing after being called names, made fun of, disrespected, dumped, threatened, she was never knocked up, beaten for the hell of it, or gang raped. One of the lucky ones, I'd say.

And in fact Kristin, having survived relatively intact, has become quite philosophical about dating. When lingering silences hang during dessert or flashes of anger creep into the bedroom, she begins planning a graceful exit that, hopefully, avoids a scene of tears, sarcasm, sharp objects, mouth-to-mouth resuscitation, or a 911 call.

Her repertoire includes "It's not you. It's me."

or the *frank* discussion of where they are and where they want to go, and where Kristin is certain of the untenable nature of their respective positions: "I want a child," to those who are overly fond of audio-video equipment and pornography, or "I don't want a child" to those who have married siblings, adoring nieces, and a sprawling barely-furnished home in the suburbs.

This is not to say that Kristin hasn't been on the receiving end of a rogue lover's disappearing act, mostly and for years by Rob who in *loving* her did more damage than crazy Jimmie ever did. And again she thinks of her first boyfriend with his hooded blue eyes and lazy way of talking.

Now they're on a porch swing gently swaying. It's a heavy summer night of calling katydids and blue moon light. With his arm around her, he pulls her close. "I love you Kristin," he says. She folds into him with welling eyes and believes those words, not just for that moment, but for years to come, seven in all.

It was an unfortunate assumption, but then those words *I love you* are not just three simple syllables pulled from the air. A better analogy would be drawn from a hat by a magician with loose lips. Ah, the trickery of rarefied words when first heard by a young girl whose experience of the world—a missing father, a lax mother, and of course the ever-hovering Jimmie, whose shenanigans were the antithesis of anything loving—we further understand how Rob became the heralding archangel to all virtue (love, truth, beauty), and how Kristin succumbed to his pretty words, not just once but a bucket of times as he roamed then returned with flowers, hickeys, and more I-love-yous.

And we are painfully reminded of our own exploits into the netherworld of romance where bondage is hardly with tape, cuffs, ropes, but with whispered words of unreliable truths spoken so sweetly. This lesson is not easy for Kristin or for any one of us. Chain of Fools. Bring it on Aretha.

The cell rings. Kristin stretches to check the ID. It's Mags. Kristin has four rings to decide if she should answer. How much baby talk can she handle? Ring two... Yesterday, little Stone had gotten into the kitty litter. Ring three... The day before he had fallen down the stairs. Not a scratch. Ring four... An ingenious question, "Mommy, why don't we have wings?" And oops, too late, the ring is silent. Kristin watches the readout. Seconds later, a message is waiting.

"Hey Kris. It's me. Just calling to see how

your day went. Stone's having SpaghettiOs. Again. He's refusing to eat anything else. What should I do? Call me."

Kristin shakes her head. She doesn't have a clue how to get a three-year-old to eat. Poor Mags.

And we, if I could make this editorial presumption, would have to likewise sympathize. Historically, there has been a great divider among women, those with child and those without, where paths separate and preoccupations, priorities jump track. Today, however, the great divide has expanded where Mags, Kristin's friend, has become a member of yet a new demographic—the single woman with child—a curious, tentative, vulnerable position where emerging micro-families break surface and bob on roiling waters where their lives, previously predictable and prone to superfluous-ness (hem lengths, caloric counts, astrology), are now imbued with generalized anxiety, confusion, and a laundry list of ailments caused by sleepless nights and rushed meals from the dollar menu.

Lately, Kristin has been on the edge of this observation as her friends expand from two camps to three. Ironically, more singles than marrieds have taken the plunge and had children. It's the married ones who are waiting. She thinks it's because couple consensus tends to take longer as pros and cons are weighed, considered, argued about, and, at some point, if not resolved, sublimated into chilly standoffs where parties abscond to separate parts of the house for scrapbooking or a thirty-second jerk off in front of the computer. Alas, family planning does have a downside. And the alternative? Kristin's brow furrows for the first time this evening.

Instead of calling her friend, she clicks on tools, summons up the calendar, and begins the calculations of counting, subtracting, adding, figuring. She is absorbed by the days of the previous weeks that must now be recalled then projected to this very day. Yes. Welcome to the secret life of women and numbers.

There's the twenty-eight-day cycle to consider if one is planning a marathon; the fourteen-day countdown plus three from the first day where caution's paramount; and the prior four days to the twenty-eight-day cycle which explains those spurts of depression, chocolate binges or debilitating cramps that feel like internal organs are being inquisitioned. And if those calculations aren't enough, sweeping modifications to the time frame, without a woman's knowledge or consent, must be further adjusted due to ignorable but potent phases of the moon, quirky hormonal bleeps, or tragically corrupted DNA helices of less robust eggs that/who, at the sac door, escape too quickly or remain stubbornly behind.

From what Kristin can figure, she is safe by a matter of few days. On the other hand, if any those little squigglies heading upstream are taking their dear sweet time, it's another matter all together. She makes a mental note to grab a pill for just such occasion. Back on track, she dials up her friend.

"Hey Mags. Just calling to check in. How's Stone doing?"

There's some shuffling. Mags's voice is distant. "Stone sweetheart, Aunt Kris wants to talk to you."

Kristin recoils certain the phone is about to be handed over. Talking to a three-year-old makes her feel stupid.

"Now Stone. Say hello to Aunt Kris."

Kristin listens. A sound like a whining cat comes through.

"Hey, Stone," Kristin says with forced animation. "Is that my boy?"

Nothing.

"Were you eating SpaghettiOs? I love those things. They're round and so delicious."

More nothing.

"You're such a big boy. But you know what? If

you want to get big and strong you got to eat dinner. Do want to be big and strong?"

"Like a car?"

"Yeah, Stone. Just like a car. Now finish up dinner, OK?"

"OK."

Seconds later, Mags is on the phone. "OMG, he's eating. What did you say to him? You're a natural. You should have kids."

"Me? I don't think so."

"Oh, Kris. It would be so much fun. We could hang out together."

Motherhood for Kristin is a minefield. How different would she be from her own mother? "Mags, get real. For one thing I don't have a boyfriend."

"Boyfriend? You don't need a frigging boyfriend. Just a donor."

"Donor?"

"You're not getting any younger."

"I'm only thirty-five."

"Time's ticking. Besides you don't want to be sixty and have a teenager. I'm thinking of having another one myself. Stone could use someone to hang out with."

Kristin's face twists up. "You are kidding, right?"

"Kidding? No. How much harder can a second baby be?"

"Do you plan on using a donor?"

There's silence on Mags's end. Kristin shakes her head. "You're not thinking of that rat?"

"He stopped over last night with the cutest stuffed bear for Stone."

"Oh Lord."

"And a bottle of wine."

Kristin sighs. "How about a check?"

"Don't be negative. So how was your day?"

Suddenly Kristin understands why Mags is her best friend. The two tend to be impulsive. "Let's see.... I went to work and fucked a guy."

"You what?"

"During lunch."

"No way."

"Way. In the stairwell."

"OMG."

"Yeah."

"Who is he?"

"I don't know. Some guy."

"Some guy? And you don't even know him? Wow."

"Yeah. It was stupid."

"Stupid? That's crazy hot. Kudos to you. Are

you seeing him again?"

"No."

"So it wasn't that good?"

Without thought, words empty out of Kristin's mouth. "Actually, it was."

"Very cool. So why don't you want to see him again?"

Kristin suddenly becomes embarrassed. "I don't know the guy. Never saw him before. I'm not even sure what he looks like."

"Get out!"

Kristin wonders. Eye color? Height? Weight? Tone of his voice? Nothing comes to mind. What's wrong with her?

And suddenly, Kristin has her first regret. Not in the act but in the telling of the act. Once a secret, nicely anchored in head space, is verbalized, it materializes, takes on form, potentiates into matter that has the possibility of gathering momentum and spinning out of control.

On the other hand, I would suggest to Kristin, keeping a secret hidden, also comes at a cost. Lies cover up secrets which generate more secrets, lies, ad infinitum, until truths are no longer recognized or told, and suddenly one becomes entrenched in a maze of uncertainty with questionable income tax returns and pending jail time.

"C'mon Kris. How could you not know what he looks like?"

"It happened kinda fast."

"Maybe. But you had to be awfully close."

"Would seem so."

Mags laughs. "Must be one of those forest-through-the-trees things."

"Clearly," Kristin says with distraction. There's a beeping on the line. "Mags, I got a call. Gotta go."

"Sure thing. You still coming over tomorrow night?"

"Yeah. See you then."

"Great. Bye."

Before answering, Kristin glances at the time. Like clockwork. She then answers the cell, "Hello, Mother."

"Krissy. Please don't call me 'mother'. You know how I hate that expression."

"But you are my mother."

"Of course. Just sounds cold."

Kristin rolls her eyes. The evening weekday phone call has been getting tiresome. When had they begun this ritual?

"Remember I was telling you about your Aunt

Barbara. Well, guess what? The purchase of the house fell through...."

Kristin pokes the fork into a noodle that's hanging over the edge of the plate. In place of her appetite, a vague but certain soft-edged stomach pang is erupting. She puts the fork down and takes a deep breath.

"....they'll just have to forget moving to Florida. Not this year. Not to mention your cousin's wedding. The sale was supposed to...."

Kristin is familiar with abdominal cramps. In fact, she has lived with them for years. After a host of doctors, procedures, medications, alternative therapies, dietary changes, her digestive tract (quirky stomach, endless yards of winding, gurgling intestines) remains a sensitive, reactive, attention-seeking system.

"Poor Jessica. I guess she'll have to downsize. You know go with carnations, look into a less expensive place. There's a gym at the town hall. It can be dressed up. Remember we went there for New Year's Eve? Plenty of room to...."

As expected, the intensity of the ache is ratcheting up. It's more of a cramp, a twisting wet towel in the general area of her solar plexus. Kristin eyes the remains of her dinner. Pasta, cream, nuts, all potential intolerances. She pushes the plate away.

"Krissy, are you listening?"

"Yes."

"Weddings these days! Who can afford them? Sheila next door. You know Sheila...."

What Kristin is vaguely aware of, but reluctant to confront, you and I may suspect. When considering the origins of bodily sensations, one should look at events immediately preceding the symptoms. Yes, she just ate dinner, but what also happened? Eureka! Her mother called. Just sayin'.

Maureen Moore, Kristin's mother, previous short-term wife to Kristin's father, long-term live-in girlfriend to Jimmie (Kristin's nemesis), and currently, the unattached woman of a certain age with few interests besides couponing and watching reality TV, is on a roll.

"....the tent was huge with seating for fifty. Anyplace can be dressed up. All you really need for a good time is plenty of food, music, and someplace to dance...."

While catching the general gist of her mother's concern for her sibling Barbara's dilemma, Kristin expects there's some sisterly tsk tsk and glee. Kristin continues to take deep breaths.

"How was your day?" her mother asks.

"Good."

"And what are you doing now?"

"Having dinner."

"What are you having?"

The pain is sharpening.

"Mom, who cares."

"Krissy, I care."

"Sorry. My stomach's bothering me."

"That stomach of yours. I just watched a show on TV about...."

Kristin wants to scream, "Shut the fuck up." But she doesn't, because she never has.

And such is the case with so many of us, born into families where everyone is floundering, trying to stay afloat, upright, in charge, grasping for any reassurance that our particular brand of collective DNA is resilient, successful, law-abiding, God-fearing, and not an embarrassment to the neighbors. When, in fact, everyone is a hot mess.

"....camomile tea...."

Kristin closes her eyes and tolerates the pain. In the background, her mother's voice is streaming nonsensical words.

So what ever happened to Jimmie? The ending was abrupt but inevitable. What Jimmie hadn't counted on was Kristin's hormones and how they fired up her pre-frontal cortex, causing an internal sea change that made her…homicidal. Particulars:

Unaware of pending doom, Maureen was in a church basement, placing markers on the B column, listening carefully for the number 9, readying her body to catapult from the chair and yell "Bingo". Meanwhile Kristin, seventeen at the time, was at home in the kitchen doing dishes with Jimmie inches away breathing down her neck, saying the usual *your-ass-needs-to-get-fucked* or some such.

The water in the sink had a billowing head of bobbing, frothy suds. She stayed focused, pulling out a glass, sponging and rinsing it, then a fork, a spoon, a plate. Feeling around for more dishes, her fingers grazed the familiar blade of the kitchen knife. And something snapped.

Dear Reader, who among us hasn't experience an unknowable moment, that middle part between before and after when the pendulum stops midair and a dramatic change of direction takes place. Such was the case with Kristin on Bingo night.

Just like now with her mother's words sounding gibberish, Jimmie's onslaught of obscenities stopped being heard. Instead, a gathering crescendo of pulsating energy powered through her body, sending an electrical current from her brain down her arm to her hand and fingers that found the knife in the lukewarm water, where it didn't feel like a knife at all, but a powerful, transforming fetish to use for protection and, possibly, salvation. In response, the frenetic rush inside her body quieted, and within the silence, she became cocooned, impregnable, calm...until a man's voice intruded, "slut". Suddenly, with knife in hand, she spun around and lunged. *En garde.*

Before going on, I must argue Kristin's defense. The attack was not premeditated. There was neither a plan nor a preceding thought, discounting previous voodoo doll incidents. It was simply a reaction having failed to react on previous occasions. Dear Reader, at some point we all must take a different road when the initial road continues to go nowhere. It's partly a matter of survival, partly a matter of horse sense. Anyway....

Jimmie's reflexes were surprisingly good. When the knife point came at him, he jumped back and immediately swung to parry the blade away. Kristin made an easy adjustment and lunge forward a second time. "You crazy bitch," he said. Kristin smiled, "Your point?" and lunged a third time. Without thought of consequences, Kristin's calm voice, an octave lower and not her own, then said,

"You want to fuck this slut's ass, drop your pants." With sweet, beautiful fear in his eyes, Jimmie's reflexes took over. His hands fell to his crotch and he backed out of the kitchen, all critical maneuvers when a woman gets really mad, has nothing to lose, and is armed.

A month later, Jimmie moved out. Maureen thought it was because she had put on a few pounds. Kristin kept her mouth shut and hoo-rahed the Jimmie era was finally over. But it wasn't the end. Not even close. Traumatic events, once past, still have teeth.

Maureen took to drinking and before long the parent/child roles reversed. Then, within the year, Jimmie had another live-in girlfriend who had an eleven-year-old daughter. Shortly thereafter, Kristin developed digestive problems.

"Krissy, are you listening. What should I do?"

"Do?"

"About the dress. Have it altered or take it back?"

"Mom, I don't know."

"What would you do?"

And a pregnant question arises.

How to explain family dynamics, where years of conditioning have led to vague, changeable, irrational rules of engagement and where we all eventually conclude the best response is no response at all.

"Mom, it's up to you."

"I know it's up to me, but what would you do?"

"I guess, I'd take it back."

"You would? But I really love the color."

"Then keep it."

"Alterations. They're not cheap. I already spent over a hundred dollars."

"Mom, return it. There are a lot of dresses out there."

"I'm just not sure if...."

And so it goes between mother and daughter, a dance of questions with answers unwanted, averted, or deluded. "Santa Claus? I'm Santa Claus." "Please don't ask about your father." "Jimmie, leave? But he loves us both."

To continue... Stomach issues aside, Jimmie's legacy of self-doubt has been churning inside Kristin for years. Doubts that she'd become a functioning member of society (Do slut's work?). Doubts that anyone would fall for her (Are sluts loveable?). Doubts that anyone would want to marry her (Are sluts brought to family dinners?). And slut-dom aside, as far of having a family of her own, what had she learned from her mother, a woman of desperate unsured-ness and questionable judgment? Not much.

They were two lost souls bobbing on open water. Grasping for life jackets from an unformalized support system of transient babysitters, disconnected family members, and men who either paid too much or too little attention. And where hopes were consistently raised, then dashed, in search of the idealized Cosby family.

"Have you responded to the wedding invitation yet?"

"No, Mom."

"What are you waiting for? You are going, right?"

Kristin sighs. When should she break the news?

"Barbara will be very disappointed."

"Mom, I hardly know Jessica."

"Krissy, she's family."

Really? Kristin thinks. Family? An occasional Christmas card? A graduation announcement? That time they accidentally bumped into each other in the mall and had nothing to say?

"Besides maybe you'll meet someone."

"At a wedding? You're supposed to bring a

date."

"Is that why you're hesitating?"

Kristin looks at the clock. A five-minute call is about all she can stand. "Listen, Mom, I need to go for a run."

After some emptiness on the line, her mother says. "All right then. Love you."

"Love you too."

Twenty minutes later, in the crepuscular glow of a setting sun, and with most of the stomach ache dissipated, Kristin is nursing a slow jog. Each step against asphalt jangles her body into alignment. As muscles tighten and release, she picks up speed. Soon she's sweating, panting, climbing an incline. Against the pull of gravity, she plows forward. Her body wants to stop, as does her mind. Fifty yards away is the crest. She must keep going.

At the top of the hill, all resistance melts. She sprints forward wildly.

+-o 6 o->

Twenty minutes after eavesdropping on his wife's conversation, Michael is at the dining room table eating a cilantro pork steak with stir-fry veggies. A second double Scotch sits beside his glass of water and the infamous flowers, unwrapped, are now taking up space on the entryway table.

Still stunned, but feeling the liquor, Michael's heartbeat is strong and steady. In record time, he has mentally evaluated the thorny situation and come up with some ideas, that is to say moves, that is to say lies, to ameliorate the situation and save himself an uncomfortable scene and/or a needless trip to see a lawyer. In tandem with the aforementioned musings, he, like a hawk, is assessing Caitlyn with new eyes, watching for who she really may be. As an aside, there's some irony here since he is both the cheating and suspicious party.

Static surrounds him that, during previous evenings, has gone unnoticed. The TV drones. Forks, knives click against the plates as his wife, daughters cut meat and poke at their food. His wife is talking to the kids, asking a lot of questions, bringing up tests, homework, barely giving them time to answer.

Michael wonders if this is normal behavior. Is she avoiding him? He makes a move to test the water. "So Babe what did you do today?" His voice sounds unconcerned. He's proud of that.

They exchange a glance. He pulls his eyes away first. A mistake. Don't be intimidated, don't show fear.

She reaches for her glass of wine. "Went through the junk drawer. Got rid of stuff."

Michael finds an opening for normalization, chit chat. "Last time I looked in there it was a hornet's nest."

"Not anymore." She's chewing, staring into space.

Yes. She's avoiding him.

Boldly, he focuses a pointed stare on her. "Did you find my folding ruler? It's been missing for months."

Her eyes cut to his. "No."

And he feels the chill.

Dear Reader, being a fly on the wall, lollygagging around, taking everything in, is a comfortable place to be. How amusing our particular vantage point is, knowing more than the familiars and watching the chess game that, while being played in full view, is rife with drama, confusion and master moves. Poor Michael. So what's his plan?

First and foremost, he's reasoned his wife knows nothing. How could she? She's simply drawing a conclusion and conclusions are often wrong or can be made wrong with more information. He's already figured a way to unsteady her assumption. But he must wait for the perfect time. Until then, he's curious if she'll bring up the Mini Cooper convertible. Which makes him take another swig of Scotch. What the hell is going on here? Blackmail? How could she do this to him? Has he not been a loving, attentive husband, a fine father, a terrific provider?

In response, he chews his food into a pulp. His jaw is tight, achy. Again he reaches for the Scotch to loosen him up, keep him in a teetering state of numbness and bravado. Swallowing a congealed glob of masticated pig meat saturated with a thirty-year-old single malt finished with a hint of oak, he tells himself everything is under control.

The conversation has now turned to shopping and when they, his wife and girls, will be going to the mall.

He sneaks a look at Caitlyn, measuring if there's any external sign of internal conflict. Perhaps strident set lips, taut and thin. Or frown lines along the mouth, worry lines between the brows. Maybe she's holding the fork, knife with a white-knuckled grasp, or shaking the foot of her crossed leg. However, except for the chilly, monosyllabic responses, he senses nothing and stares off.

To imagine his wife has known of his indiscretions and not gone into an hysterical rant is, well, off-putting. Why so accommodating? Is what's good for the goose, game for the gander? And he wonders about those girls' night-outs, drunk parties at the neighbors, hang-up calls when he answers. Has he been paying up while she's been playing around? There's something intrinsically unfair when two people don't play by the same rules, he oddly thinks.

His daughter is talking to him. "Daddy, are you listening?"

"Sorry Pumpkin. What did you say?"

"Why did you buy Mom flowers?"

Alleluia. The seas part and the moment has arrived. Before answering, he waits until everyone is looking directly at him. "I have a confession to make."

Caitlyn's fork is hanging midair. His two daughters are stock still.

"I had an ulterior motive."

His wife's face seems to be draining of color.

Knowing a beautiful finesse is about to be played, he lingers. Yes. Michael is a sporting man at the ready to cast aside caution, fear, and move intrepidly forward where other men fall behind. That, or he is getting quite drunk.

"Well, not exactly an ulterior motive. Just killing two birds with one stone. Sorry Babe."

Her brow furrows. "What are you talking about?"

"The flowers. I sent them as a favor. Not a favor to you but a favor to one of my clients."

"If the flowers weren't for me, why were they delivered here? Why was my name on them? And the card." Her voice is strained.

"Babe, they were for you. I sent them. It's just that one of my clients was telling me about his uncle's flower shop. It's not doing well. I figured I'd throw some business his way."

Caitlyn slumps into the chair.

"Are you disappointed?"

She looks at him. Is that a hint of a smile? "No. Of course not."

From Michael's perspective, the basket has been made, the goal scored, and he just saved himself the cost of an overpriced British bumper car. Now to watch the impact. A sweet smile is nice, but shouldn't she feel guilty having made an assumption about him cheating? Shouldn't she be apologetic in some way realizing she has maligned him to her sister? Or would that be asking too much?

If I may interject...yes, Michael, that would be asking too much. Don't push your lying luck. Be happy and learn from the situation. Get on your knees and thank whatever force has protected your sorry ass.

Caitlyn is now collecting the dishes. "Who'd like ice cream?"

In unison, they all say, "Me."

"OK," she says. "Two chocolates and one pistachio with hot fudge coming up".

Inwardly celebrating, Michael beams. The rough patch is over, and he can now savor the swirling green melting concoction that is his trademark. "Sounds great Babe." He reaches for her arm. She leans into him and allows a kiss. Remarkably, Michael forgets everything—the earlier dalliance, the overheard phone conversation, the mind-boggling machinations of a cheating husband.

Dear Reader, there are those in this world who have remarkable gifts. Those impresarios who orchestrate events; those actors who inhabit characters; those visionaries who see beyond the veil. And let's not forget those jack rabbits, like Michael, who run like hell over branches and brambles always reaching their destination unscathed. Bravo.

Three hours later, Michael and Caitlyn are in the bedroom. To assuage his guilt and any lingering doubt on Caitlyn's part, Michael moves in to seal the deal, that is to say make love, have sex. He takes it particularly slow.

As she removes her jewelry in the dresser mirror, he stands behind her. They are looking at each other in the reflection. He untucks her shirt, slips beneath and wraps his hands around her waist. She's warm, soft.

"We've been invited to a cookout next door.

Sunday around 6," she says.

He kisses her neck. "Sounds good."

"Up for doing ribs?"

"No problem."

"Great. I'll let Ann know."

She twists around. They are face to face. "You're sweet." And she moves in to his mouth. First nibbling, then teasing his lips with a little bite.

Which makes Michael wonder, is she feeling guilty after all? Perhaps so. He decides to run with it, hold back a little, and have her take charge.

She doesn't disappoint. She fiddles with her clothes, strips down, then does the same to him. Soon they are standing almost naked. Almost. Her hand is down his boxers. He's rubbing her tits, placing a finger inside her. Her hand is playful with a light touch. He wants to fuck her but is waiting to see how far she'll go. He's thinking it would be nice to have her kneel and come down on him. To make things easier he slips out of his underwear and stays standing. She continues to stroke his penis.

Dear Reader, what goes on in bedrooms gets complicated when the parties rely on nuance, wordless expectation to spearhead the crescendo of rising heat. Many assume that because they are naked, in the same place at the same time, and touching each other, their communal experience is one. But alas it rarely is. Usually it's two people in their own minds experiencing their own bodies becoming particularly self absorbed with the mounting physical reaction exacerbated/tempered by bio-chemicals, emotional baggage, interior replays, troubling propensities, strident religious acculturation (guilt, fear, blindness), and the worry of the way their bodies look, taste, smell. Yes, Michael wants a blow job, but will he say so? No. In his book, communication is for dummies and, on this particular evening, he suffers the consequences. His wife guides him to the bed and slips beneath him.

In a few moments, he attempts to enter but she's not quite ready, not quite hot enough. And a little dry. With some manipulation, he guides his penis inside her. After two pumps, it slips out. A second and third attempt, bring more slippage. What's going on here? The realization hits. His primal, king-of-the-jungle force is slowly, but decidedly retreating, checking out, shriveling up. He changes position and tries one more time.

"What's wrong?" Caitlyn asks.

"Nothing. I don't know. Maybe I drank too much."

This hasn't happened before. Not like this. Not when all systems were go. To draw attention away from the situation, he rubs her the way she likes and tells her she's beautiful. She responds. A few minutes later, spooned together, she asks. "Why didn't you kiss me when you came home?"

"Huh?"

"When you came home. You didn't give me a kiss."

"Oh. Right. I had onions for lunch. I needed to brush my teeth."

Dear Reader, onions? Did you read *onions*? Did I write *onions*? And suddenly we know Michael's goose is cooked.

***

For the past hour, Kristin has been in an odd place. After the intense run and subsequent shower, she's pulled a chair over to the front window, thrown up the sash, and is now sitting in the dark, watching the evening turn black. The TV's off. There's no music.

Something's not quite right. She feels untethered, swoony, not necessarily bad, more like some interior alignment has shifted; like she's a bit stoned.

She closes her eyes. The breeze is soft, pillowlike against her cheek. A rickety, rhythmic cycling is heard. She listens, isolating the chain as it locks into the circling teeth, the chime of metal against metal, the rubber as it glides across asphalt. And yes, there's the air. It's streaming, like colored ribbons, across and around the skeletal, aerodynamic surfaces of merged metal, rubber, polymers.

To confirm what she hears and imagines, her eyes open. The cyclist, a dark shadow who is weaving down the block getting caught in a patch of street light to then disappear and reappear again, captures her interest, anchors her to a tangible spot. She lets out a calming sigh. Her mind has been racing for hours, dipping into memories, conflicted feelings, where she's been looking into a cracked mirror and seeing sharp, fractured parts of herself.

Dear Reader, Kristin is not alone. How any of us can fathom who we truly are, our wholeness, amid the morass of indoctrination tossed our way by, to name a few: trippy, old, dead people; newly-hatched sycophants of 5th Avenue; loving, but equally confused, blood relations; and everything our limited senses absorb and wrongly interpret. Yes, we survive, but it's in a walking-wounded state of reactive parts. In other words, "Kristin, you are not alone."

But she is alone, she's certain. Alone in her slut-dom where no one has lived her life. Where it's not whether she is or isn't a slut, but to what degree she finds herself on the slut-dom scale of one to ten on any particular day, rain or shine. And today, she's reached a new high, a rare ten; a ranking where she should be given a crown of thorns and dragged around a courtyard, naked, ashamed, with toothless crowds jeering. Who fucks a stranger in the middle of the day at work for chrissake? Her voice is weak. "I do." And oddly, she smiles. Now I understand her predicament. She's in a place that feels good and bad at the same time. Major mind fuck.

Conflicted feelings grow roots. Love OR hate completely and there's no confusion. Love AND hate and you are trapped in an endless loop of retreat/attack, kiss/bite, and salvaging something you just threw into the garbage. It's the kind of thing that short circuits your brain by sending mixed messages to and from the amygdala that then run rampant hither and yon, sparking enough friction and heat to blow out an EEG. Hyperbole? Perhaps. The point is, ambivalent feelings cause resistant plexus tangles, defiant to remediation or undoing.

As witnessed by Kristin where after she

reframed the initial guilt, shame, worn out tears, she concluded being a slut had some advantages. With the mantle of slut, she no longer had to be nice. Anger seeped out of her. Attention and power followed. Attention to what she wore, how she looked, and the power of words repeated—calling other girls names and seeing them whimper in the principal's office. But most of all she had power over Jimmie. As her clothes got tighter, his eyes got hungrier, his words viler. But that was fine because it gave her a reason to be angry, to not be such an innocent, to spit out any crap other people threw at her. It seemed a fair bargain. I take, I give. And she was released from being vulnerable, that weakness of a simpering little girl who cried for stupid things, like seeing a kitten tossed across a room.

Kristin didn't know she was playing with fire. Not only with Jimmie but with her psyche. She was joining the party, plowing over the fine lines that separated offender and offendee. All the while gorging powerful emotions into a huge ball of snarled feelings where no matter how much power or attention she had, there were aftershocks with Richter scales through the roof. Slut-dom became woven into her persona leaving her to question her intelligence, her beauty, her assets, if there were any.

Then came the denial. Denial for anything she deserved, denial to fall in love, denial to think of herself other than a selfish, self-centered bitch who no one liked, who she didn't like.

Then this afternoon happened. Another act of slutiness without guilt, without caring, and now this confusion over those damn words with their magical pull. "Lets' fly."

Dear Reader, Kristin's heart is racing again, feeling on the cusp of some epiphany. But it slips away. In its place she thinks she's got to make some changes before she gets to be the kind of slut she has never considered—an old slut.

Twenty minutes later she's in bed. Her body jerks as if she's falling. She wills herself to stay steady. She's on a highwire. Darkness is around her. The only direction is straight ahead, but where does it lead? Maybe she should jump or turn back or not move at all. Considering the options, she also remembers the pill. She must get that pill. But welcome sleep is descending upon her. She'd take it in the morning. No problem.

+-o 7 o->

At 2 PM the following afternoon, we are waiting in the cafeteria, where 24 hours earlier, Michael and Kristin met. We are curious to see what will happen. We are voyeurs, comfortably reading, allowing our own lives to fade into the background. Shamelessly, albeit discretely, smugly, we slip into the fictive dream, anticipating another intersection of paths, another bout of colliding lips, another train wreck.

While we hover in the lunchroom, Michael remains in his office. He has been watching the clock, the minutes as they pass. He is desperately aware there are windows of opportunity, that when not opened, slam shut. He would like to see the woman again but at what cost? He's not thinking of his family but of his ego. Would he be able to perform?

Several floors away, at her desk, Kristin is eating a lunch packed earlier: a carton of whole milk, a tuna fish sandwich on multigrain bread. Between sips and bites, she searches online, absorbing as much as she can about the dietary recommendations for the first trimester.

And so goes one ending.

Another occurs sixteen months later.

Riding in a racing green Mini convertible, Michael and Caitlyn are heading west on I90. It's a fall day in western New York. The top is down and Michael is completely enthralled by the speed of the car, the wind in his face, and the blur of the fall colors. It's a week-end trip to several wineries. And his marriage?

A couple of days after the flower incident, Caitlyn brought up the Mini Cooper. Realizing she wasn't fooled, he formulated a follow-up plan of least resistance. Since she had remained silent and continued to sleep in the same bed, he figured fair play was whatever they agreed on, verbalized or not. And it was off to the car dealership.

He thinks of the woman, the firmness of her flesh beneath the skin, the surprising force of her body. But most of all he remembers the beauty of the anonymity of it, not knowing anything about her, not wanting to know anything about her. She was a passing indescribable scent that left him desiring more, but knowing if there were more the experience would become mundane. It's the stepping out of the routine that makes it special. First times, only times, are the best times when done properly. It's the exhilaration. The flight.

Kristin is at home on this same Saturday. She never was pregnant. (Unknown to her Michael had had a vasectomy years earlier.) After a month, she made two changes in her life. First, she went to the animal shelter and got a puppy, something to care for and be cared about. Second, she bought an Electra Verse 21-speed bike to soar downhill. These simple acts retraced steps she had skipped along the way and put her on track to self-understanding and forgiveness that had gotten waylaid.

Kristin entered a tunnel that day at work and came out a reclaimed person. It had to do with being free. Free from the endless trash talk, free from the degradation, lies, hurt. And where, for once, her sexuality, released from tangled tethers, was recast in the light of exploration and discovery. Removing the chains of the past and spreading her wings, soon followed.

Now, the final ending. Yours and mine.

Dear Reader, there are dimensions here, levels of existence, spheres of energy, if you like, where stories reflect some realities up for interpretation. This being said, it was my plan to entice you with sex, to hold your interest, to keep you on the line. In the end, however, it was about me and my theory of our communal journey and transcendence across dimensions. "Let's fly."

About the Author:

Linda A. Lavid is an award-winning writer and artist from western New York. She is widely published. To learn more, visit:

lindalavid.com

Other Books by Linda A. Lavid:

Rented Rooms: A Collection of Short Fiction
Paloma: A Laurent & Dove Mystery
Thirst: A Collection of Short Fiction
Composition: A Fiction Writer's Guide for the 21st Century
Weekly Strategies for Writers
On Creative Writing (E-Book only)
Spots Blind: Short Stories
101 Ways to Meditate: Discover Your True Self
Of the Dance/De la Danza: Bilingual Stories